A

A Poetry Collection

Keyley Pickard

Table of Contents

Dedication

To my family and friends who believed in me even when

didn't.

Acknowledgements

Chris Martin and Big Boy, two besties who always told

me to keep it up and push forward.

About the Author

Born Keyley Marie Pickard, Sept. of '85, I have two children, also a fur baby mama, am married as well. I love to write and spend time with my children and fur babies. I love sports and music as well, but most of all my writing and babies.

Introduction

Poems written during the years 1996-2018

Bits and pieces of these poems were written during a rough time in my life after my best friend committed suicide. Others were written when a friend was murdered and some when I had my children. Being a mother of two, the poetess in me has also sought inspiration from watching my children, listening to them as well.

Poem No: 01 'Imagined'

Never did I imagine I'd find someone as sweet as you. I never imagined I'd fall in love with you. Never did I imagine I'd fall for someone so loving. Fall for someone so caring. I don't know what I'd do without you now. Waking up to you, to your smile, to your touch; waking up with you by my side... Never had I imagined. Someone so sweet. Someone so loving, kind and caring. Never did I imagine I'd find someone as sweet as you Every time I hear you say you love me, it sends chills down my spine. Every time I hear your voice, it sends chills all over my body. Seeing your smile... Seeing your face... Never had I imagined.

Poem No: 02 'Forbidden Love'

Memories may fade, time may stop, but for me the happily ever after shall never come. These dreams I dream are nothing more than forbidden love, forbidden future I hope for. My heart bleeds for the love I seek. My soul breaks with the lies. The pain that never goes away. A happily ever after that will never be known. Ghosts haunting me, of the forbidden love. On my own, on my knees; no hero to save me. These dreams I dream of my hero, my knight in shining armor are nothing more than forbidden love, forbidden future I long for. In pieces, my heart stops, my belief stops in this world. Have I lost it all? Have I lost the only thing in this silent world? On my own down this lonely world of the unknown, in forbidden love with the one that left me in the silence of the wind. Memories may fade, time may stop; a happily ever after shall never come. My heart bleeds in the silence of the night. The night sky darkens the moonlight hidden like forbidden dreams, forbidden love, the forbidden future.

The pain never goes away, my soul burns, but I am one the only one in this lonely place. A happily ever after that will never be known. Ghosts haunting me, of forbidden love. On my own, on my knees; no hero to save me. I'm waiting for that love that will never come, a love that I hold close. My heart bleeds, my soul breaks with these lies; the pain that never goes away

Poem No: 03 'Survivor'

She's a survivor;
No matter how much you try to sink her
You can not win
You can either turn around and walk away
or she will turn on you
She's a survivor;
Nothing can or will keep her down
Her head held high
A skip in her step
Queen of the darkness, she may be.
But she still seeks a little light from all this evil
No matter how much you try and destroy her
She's always a survivor
You will never win
You can either turn around and walk away or
she will turn on you
She will live forever
'Cause she's the queen of the darkness

Poem No: 04 'The Truth'

For the truth shall arise
As the sun sets
Darkness falls on deaf ears, as she falls from grace with broken wings
Your lips speak lies and hate
Your open arms speak of destruction
As she falls from grace with broken wings
The angel you once knew torn to pieces
Ripped to shreds, lost in the darkness.
For the truth shall arise as she stands in the shadows of the night
Will you run for your life
With your lips that speak lies and hate
Will you run and hide
With your open arms of destruction
As darkness falls on deaf ears, she falls from grace with broken wings
The truth speaks
The angel no more, now torn to pieces
Ripped and lost in the darkness
As the truth seeks the light

Poem No: 05 'My World... Upside Down'

The scent of you lingering where I sleep
Darkness creeping over me
Smiles plague my lips
So close but yet so far away
For your soul I pray
My world turned upside down as you destroy what once was
Evilness plagues the room
As I fall from grace
The scent of you lingering where you once stood
The fire in my eyes turns to black as night
As you turn my world upside down.
No tears shall I cry
Evil conquers all who are in the room
So close but yet so far away
For your soul I pray
My world turned upside down as you destroy what once was
As I fall from grace
The fire in my eyes turns to black as night.

Poem No: 06 'Addiction'

My addiction
How can I tell you just what you do to me?
All these empty, lonely nights
You're my addiction
One I can't lose
Your touch gets me high
The smile that plagues your lips gets me drunk
Don't be stupid, this is real
You're the better part of me
My great addiction
Standing on the edge
Showing the best I can to what is real
How can I prove this is me
This is what I want, what I crave
My addiction
No more empty, lonely nights
Your body, mind and soul gets me high
Drunken bliss in your presence
You're the better part of me.

Poem No: 07 'Laugh... Deep Inside'

Oh, you poor sweet thing
How I laugh
What sacrifice has one made
Fear is only in your mind
And it has taken over
What sacrifice has one made
Oh yeah, yeah, so sweet, so innocent
Don't make me laugh anymore
You couldn't sacrifice yourself if it meant saving your
mother.
Fear is all you feel
Try and hide it all you want
Try and deny it, we see through it
You live and breathe through the lies you've made and
told
Do you think we are stupid
Oh yeah yeah, so sweet, so innocent
What sacrifice has one made
Fear is in your heart
Fear is all you see and feel
Don't make me laugh
Oh, how I laugh deep inside
It's taking over you.

Poem No: 08 'Betrayal'

You said she was your everything
She meant everything to you
Lies is all you told.
You said she was the most beautiful woman
You said she was all you wanted, all you ever needed.
From sunrise to sunset, all it was, was lies.
You said you loved her for the fight she had in her
You said you loved her for the love and support she always gave
Lies is all that slipped between your lips.
You said you'd lay down your own life for her
You said she was everything to you
From sun up to sun down, lies poured out your mouth.
Foolishness she knew, but trust is what she had, love is what she wanted
You said she was your everything
She meant the whole world to you.
But lies, betrayal, is all you really gave her.

Poem No: 09 'Fairy Tales'

I used to believe in love and fairy tales
I used to believe in happy endings and ever afters
But love breaks your heart
Love destroys all you have in the end.
I used to believe in one and onlys
Prince Charming and all that I used to believe in, but what was once a dream has now become a lost cause.
I used to believe in all, until the broken hearts, broken promises and everything in between.
Now my blood runs cold, freezing my heart, changing my mind
Fairy tales, happy endings, ever afters are nothing more than a child's dreams.
Dreams of love, prince charming, a white picket fence, nothing more than a dumb girl's wishes.
Through it all, I've learned never to trust another man again.
Time will only tell where I go from here,
but hell, here I come.

Poem No: 10 'Sweet Child'

Do not hang your weary head, sweet child
For morrow is just around the corner
For as morrow breaks, the sun kisses your sweet face
As the wind blows gently through your hair, singing its
happiest song.
Do not hang your weary head, sweet child
For 'tis a blessed day
Do rise and smile, for you are loved with all hearts of
hearts.
Bare feet running down the hall
Filling the house with laughter
For morrow is just another day, around the corner filled
with joy and happiness.
Do not hang your weary head, sweet child
Rise and smile with love, joy, and happiness
And remember, you are loved with all hearts of hearts.

*To Jaxon, my dearest son. Smile and the world will smile
with you.*

Poem No: 11 'Good Enough'

I feel that I'm never going to be good enough for you
Your expensive clothes, fancy cars
Now I know I'll never be good enough
I can't believe I ever thought I could be good enough
Never should I have imagined I'd ever fit in.
But I can't let go
I can't say no to you
My heart, body, mind and soul crave you
Crave your sweet words.
I may be dreaming, but I now know I'll never be good
enough for you.
I can't say no to you
I've lost myself in this dream completely of wanting,
needing you
Your expensive clothes, fancy cars
Never should I have imagined I'd ever fit in,
Never should I have thought I was good enough for you
to love me the way I love you
I just can't let go
I can't say no to you
Craving your sweet words, your tender touch
Never will I be good enough.

Poem No: 12 'My Mind'

The sun rises and sets with you on my mind
Here I sit, knowing it will never change
Alone, your lies rolling through my mind
I was never good enough for you
The stars above shine down upon my broken soul
The moon lights up my torn heart
Here I sit all alone, wondering why all the lies…
Lesson learned,
Trust gone.
What if the tables were turned?
The sun rises and sets with you on my mind.
I gave you more of me than you deserved
Now I regret falling for your deceiving ways
The stars above shine down upon my broken soul
The moon lights up my torn heart
Torn to pieces, broken to pieces because of you.
Lesson learned as I sit alone under the blue moon.

Poem No: 13 'Time Ticks'

Time ticks by as I sit alone. Am I dreaming? Tell me I'm dreaming.

All these thoughts pouring through my mind as I sit alone on the edge of this cliff

Knowing now we were never one. Knowing now you'll never return to me

I can't help but wonder. Was I ever good enough for you

I can't help but wonder. Was I truly what you wanted?

Time ticks by as I sit here alone, wondering if it was all lies like before.

The fights, the arguing. What was it all for, if you just leave like you did

Am I dreaming? Tell me I'm dreaming. What were we working for if it wasn't real? Knowing now we were never one. Knowing now you'll never return to me

I can't help but wonder. Was I ever good enough? I can't help but wonder

Was it all lies again? What if it was true? What if the fights and arguing were something? You know I love you. You know I am nothing without you by my side. Time ticks by as I sit alone. Am I dreaming? Tell me I'm dreaming.

Please tell me you still love me. Tell me all these fights weren't for nothing in the end. Time ticks by as I sit alone with my tears, with my thoughts.

No, I'm not dreaming. Yes, this is real. All alone, no more you and I.

Poem No: 14 'Boo, My love'

Ye so sweet
One so loving
Thy dearest friend
Thy dearest boo
For ye love so tender
Thee smile so sweet
So pure and true
One hast merely captivated my heart
Thou 'tis grateful for thee
Do not hang your head, boo
For this be a thank you for ye hast done
For the love and support ye hast given unto me.
One so sweet as thee, one so loving as thee
'Tis my pleasure to know thee, to love thee as one hath
done for me.
Thy dearest friend
Thy dearest boo
So pure and true I doth love thee, my beloved boo.

Poem No: 15 'Awake'

I lie awake at night wondering is it all worth it?
What are we really fighting for?
What if at the end, it was for nothing?
I've worked so hard to get where I am and where I want
to be, but in the end, is it worth it?
I lie awake at night wondering if it's true?
I am nothing without you
But the time passes and you are not near
Are we just fooling ourselves?
What are we really fighting for?
But in the end, is it worth all the pain we've endured?
I am nothing without you by my side, hand in hand
My heart is empty knowing you are not near
You said forever and I believed it
I lie awake at night wondering is it all really worth it?
Is it worth it?
You are worth it all.

Poem No: 16 'Scars'

She hides her scars from the world
But you see right through her
You see her for who she truly is, for what she is
You accept her with flaws and all
She hides her tears from the world
The mask never reveals what is truly on her face
The cover of glasses over her eyes never truly show what
her eyes will tell.
She hides her fear so no one knows she's scared to lose
you
Her heart sinks when you aren't near
Trying to take it one day at a time
Her scars run deep and wide
But you see right through her
She keeps her heart under lock and key and the only key
she had given to you
She hides no more
She lets her scars show and wears them proudly
For you have opened her up to a whole new world
A world of love, trust, compassion.
You have proven to her what it truly means to be loved
She hides no more.

Poem No: 17 'Fear'

Time has no meaning when fear is taking over all the time
Dry those eyes darling, and show no fear
Lying there, write it out
Fear and sorrow holding tightly
Nothing else seems to matter
Dead of the night, the thunder rolls and lightning lights the sky
Shadows dancing along the walls as fear takes over
Dry those tears darling, fear is only an emotion,
An emotion you can overcome
Shadows dancing along the walls
Time has no meaning when fear is taking over all the time.

Poem No: 18 'Come to Me'

Come to me, Hold her close. She wakes with tears; who was He. Why was she seeing him? She cries, her heart aches. The stars shine down, through the dark cloudy night sky. Come to me, He cries for her. He screams for her. She's so confused. Tears fall like waterfalls. Love, hate, heartbreak. Why was she feeling this way? Who was he she was seeing in her dreams? Why does he keep telling her to go to him? *Come to me.*

Poem No: 19 'Heart and Soul'

Stars brightly shining down upon us.
Lighting our way back to one another.
Oceans apart, miles away and yet our hearts, our souls connect as one.
For in the time of need, our souls know
For in a time of pain and sorrow, our hearts cry for the other.
Stars brightly shining down upon us.
Lighting our way to one another
Searching for the smile we once had
Searching for what we once loved
Oceans apart, miles away, and yet we connected as one
When you smile, I smile
When you laugh, I laugh
Hand in hand, heart to heart, soul for soul, one we have become again.
One we shall always be.

Poem No: 20 'Much Love'

I love you so much. My love for you will never fade away. Standing next to you hand in hand is all I dream of. Baby, I've fallen madly deeply in love with you. I stand looking in the mirror, and all I see is you and me. My heart beats for you. You pick me up when I've fallen. You hold me tight and never let go. It will always be your love for me that gets me through the rough times. It will always be your smile I see. Your embrace overpowers everything. Don't let me go, take me as yours and only yours. Here in the darkness, I know I'm not alone. Don't let me go. My love for you is true and strong. You pick me up when I have fallen, true and deep, never let me go. My love for you shall never fade. As time passes, it shall become stronger and never shall you stand alone. Your warm embrace powers it all. It will always be your smile I see. My heart and soul are yours and yours alone.

Poem No: 21 'My Hand'

Take my hand into yours and show me the world
Wrap your arms around my waist, hold me tight
Never let me go
Never let me fall
Take my hand into yours and show me the world
Wrap me up tightly in your arms and show me what true
love is
Take me to higher places
Take me to all new levels of love
Never let me go
Never let me fall to no return
Show me all of you
Take my hand into yours and show me the world.

Poem No: 22 'Unconditional'

The love I have for you is deep, true and unconditional.
My heart belongs to you
My soul is yours for all eternity
My mind and body are yours always and forever.
Your smile makes me weak in the knees
Your voice makes my heart skip a beat every time it hits my ears.
Any time you are near, my body trembles
The love I have for you is deep, true and unconditional
Time may be pushing on, but my heart stands still waiting, wanting, needing you.
My heart belongs to you
You hold my heart in your hands
My soul is yours for all eternity
Be gentle and love me unconditionally.

Poem No: 23 'Anyone'

Does anyone hear her cries?
Does anyone really see the pain she hides?
She's made mistakes
She's tried to do what's best
But does anyone truly care what's going on with her?
She cries on the inside, she fakes her smiles
No one truly knows her
No one truly cares
She screams for help
Can anybody hear her?
The wounds run deep
The heartbreak kills her
She walks out the door.
She doesn't want to hurt anymore
Can't help the way she feels
She can't help; no one truly cares.

Poem No: 24 'Don't Walk Out That Door'

Don't walk out that door. Don't walk away from me. The emptiness creeps in quickly. Take me with you, don't leave me. Misery without you; hatred towards you. My heart has always been yours, and you shatter it into a million pieces. You say always and forever. Don't walk out that door. Don't walk away from me. Misery, shattered into pieces, tell me who you are. You're not who I fell in love with. Emptiness creeps in quickly. Take me with you, don't leave me. Misery without you. Hatred towards you. But yet I love you so much I can't be without you.

Poem No: 25 'Broken, Tears'

She's more broken than anyone knows, stronger on the outside than she is on the inside. Every memory brings tears to her eyes. The smiles, the laughter you see, fake. Her cries reach the night sky, weakness she can not show. Her wounds were covered for protection. Standing shattered into pieces standing before your eyes. Can you not see it? Can you not hear her cries?

Tears burning her eyes, memories burn in her thoughts. Is she alive? Her wounds opened further. No sunlight, no bright side to her future. She's more broken than anyone knows, stronger on the outside than she is on the inside. Every memory brings tears to her eyes. The smiles and the laughter you see are all fake. Her cries reach to the night sky. Weakness she cannot show. Her wounds were covered for protection.

Poem No: 26 'Unforgiven, Forbidden'

Dream the dream of happiness, love and forgiveness
The dream that can never be
The unforgiven dream
The forbidden dream
What is happiness without love and forgiveness?
There is no happiness, no love, no forgiveness
She dreams an unforgiving dream
She dreams of forbidden happiness, love and forgiveness
She dreams of being in his arms, held tight
Dreaming of their forbidden love, happiness and forgiveness
The unforgiving dream
She dreams of being his one and only
The forbidden dream
What is happiness without love and forgiveness
The dream that can never be
Forbidden.

Poem No: 27 'No Faith'

No faith in her
What is love without faith?
No trust in her
What is love without trust?
Without faith and trust there is no hope;
Without faith and trust there is no love.
You say you trust her
You say you have faith in her
You have said over and over you love her
But do you really?
Time and time again, over and over, hasn't she proved
herself?
Right, wrong, yeah things mess up
Right or wrong, doesn't she prove herself?
Doesn't she show her true colors?
Right or wrong, doesn't she do enough, her best?
No faith in her
No true trust
There is no true love for her.

Poem No: 28 'Thinking'

Sitting here thinking to myself, why you?
Why do I love you?
Why do I think about you all the time?
Telling myself that this isn't true.
Asking myself why I never told you just how much
I loved you.
Sitting here thinking to myself, how I could never really
Tell you how I feel.
Why do I love you so much?
Things like this aren't supposed to happen when I am also
In love with someone else.
Sitting here trying to figure out why I have never told you
Any of this before?

Poem No: 29 'Is Love'

Love is love
When you love someone as much as
I love you.
Expressing it is kind of hard to do.
Loving you is the only thing that gets me through the day.
You may only be my daughter, but words cannot describe
how much I love you.
Love just isn't love.
Love is kindness.
Love is caring.
Love is compassion.
Love is something you have to learn how to do.
Loving you is the only thing that gets me through the day.

To my daughter Mackenzy, with love from Mommy <3

Poem No: 30 'Dream'

Dreaming a dream
When I dream, it all seems real.
But dreams are nothing.
If dreams were something, then you would be
With me.
If dreams meant anything, then you would be
Sitting here next to me.
Dreaming is something people do to psych themselves
out.
Dreaming a dream
Wishing you were still here with me.
Best friends
Best friends forever, no matter what has happened.
Dreaming a dream of you and me together again.

Poem No: 31 'Pass By'

Watching the clouds pass by.
Listening to the wind in the trees.
Wondering if you are up there watching down on me?
Wondering are you trying to tell me something?
As I sit here outside, watching these clouds pass by
And listening to the wind
in the trees, I wonder
What do you look like today?
Wondering what you would be doing with your life
If you were here?
Watching the clouds pass by.
Listening to the wind in the trees.

Poem No: 32 'Night, My Little Angels'

Ni-night, It's night night time. Lay your head down on your pillow. Close your eyes, Dream sweet dreams, Mommy's little angels, it's ni-night time.

Close those eyes, Go to sleep and dream away, my precious

little babies, it's ni-night time. Ni-night

It's night night time. Lay your heads down upon your pillows

Close your eyes, Dream sweet dreams

May the angels of the East, West, North and South, watch over your precious

sweet dreams. Good night my angels.

To my angels Mackenzy and Jaxon with love from Mommy <3

Poem No: 33 'Time Again...'

Time and time again, we wondered what would have become of us if things had been any different.

Wondering what life would have been like if we had worked everything out.

Time and time again, I have to wonder what you are feeling about our "Friendship"?

Now knowing if this is love I feel for you

Or if it's just a "Friendship" feeling?

Time and time again, I've wondered what would have become of us if things were different.

Poem No: 34 'So Hard'

Trying so hard to show you just how much I love you.
Trying to show you with every fiber of my being, my body
Just how much you mean to me.
Loving you oh so very much.
When I hear your voice, my whole body tingles.
When I see you, I get butterflies in my stomach.
Trying so hard to show you how much I love you.
Trying to show you with every fiber of my being, my body,
Just how much you truly mean to me.
Loving you, needing you, wanting to be with you.
Your smile, your laugh, the sparkle in your eyes.
Trying so hard to be the woman you truly deserve.

Poem No: 35 'Days and nights'

The days and nights without you burn heavy on my heart.
Like we'll never return to what we had before.
When you're gone, I'm broken into a million pieces and just
When I think I can pick up
Those pieces, they all fall apart again.
Breathing, living without you just isn't an option.
It's tearing me apart being without you.
Your voice, to say 'Good morning,' your voice to say 'Good night.'
Or 'I love you.'
My heart can't take it anymore.
The days and nights without you burn heavy on my heart.
Wishing to be in your arms once again.

Poem No: 36 'Temporary'

Time and time again, I remind myself that this is only temporary.

Time and time again, I have to remind myself of what we had

Before all this.

I close my eyes and try to dream of us together once again.

I dream of your smile, of your voice, your lips pressed against mine.

My heart aches for you.

My body and soul needs you

Remembering what we had is easy.

Keeping what we have is hard.

I close my eyes and dream about you every night and day.

Dreaming about everything about you and I, missing everything

We once had.

I remind myself time and time again that this, what it is now is

Only temporary.

Poem No: 37 'My One and Only'

My one and only love
Love the way you make me smile
Love the way you make me laugh
Always and forever will I be your Queen and you'll
Be my King.
The way you smile
The way you laugh
Everything about you I love.
Miss having your arms wrapped around me tightly
Miss your sweet hugs, you loving tender kisses, my
King, my love, my only love.
When I'm with you, nothing else matters
The only love for me is your love,
My one and only love.

Poem No: 38 'Wanna Feel'

Wanna feel your body on top of mine.
Wanna feel your hands running along my hips.
Need to feel your touch.
Looking into your eyes, smiling says it all.
You wanna love me
You need to love me
Feeling your hands all over my body
Needing you to take me
Take me on the floor
Take me on the table.
Take me anywhere, as long as I'm with you, nothing
Is better than being with you.
Boy, all I need is you.
Everything about you is what I need, what I want.
Wanna feel your body pressed to mine.
Feeling your lips against my skin.
Feeling your hands caress my body.
Wanna feel your body on top of mine.
Wanna feel your hands running along my hips.

Poem No: 39 'Saved Her'

You think you saved her.
But all you did was kill her inside.
You think you love her
But she's frozen because of you
She can't love.
She stands with a burning match
Smiles sweetly, burns it to the ground
You think you know her
You have no clue what you did to her.
She stands screaming, "Burn, burn to the ground."
You thought you saved her
You thought you loved her, when you just killed her.
Nothing you do can save her.
Your lies, your smug smiles, your fake 'I love yous'
You killed her.

Poem No: 40 'Loved Her'

You say you love her
You say she's all you need
But you lie
You cheat.
You play with her emotions
You play with her heart
Don't lie to her
Don't play with her emotions
Don't play with her heart.
If you truly love her, hold her tight and
Never let go
If she's all you truly need, show her,
Don't play games.
Be true to her, as she is always true to you
She's always been true to you
You say you love her, but show her no love
You say she's all you'll ever need, but yet you
Play games.
You say you love her, that you need her;
There she lays all alone yet again.

Poem No: 41 'Pain'

She's crying out in pain
Can't you see what's happened to her?
Can't anyone hear her screams?
The love she showed must mean nothing to you.
The caring, kindness of her heart she showed you
Must mean nothing.
Playing games with her heart
Crying out in pain
Trying not to show how hurt she really is.
Can't anyone see she's lost faith in all things love?
Can't anyone tell she's bleeding on the inside? Can't you
hear her cries for help?
You broke her heart for the last time.
She trusted you for the last time
It's time to say good-bye and quit playing games with
Her heart.
It's time to move on and say good-bye
She gave you all of her
And you played too many games with her.

Poem No: 42 'Hatred'

These feelings of hatred won't go away.
I hate the way I feel for you.
I dislike the way I gave you every part of me
I don't miss you
I don't miss the way you treated me
These feelings of your death keep rushing over me
These images of the way you left this world, racing
Through my mind.
I laugh at your pain
Hate everything about you
Keep telling myself I never really loved you.
Keep telling myself that the love I truly have for you
Is really hatred.
But it isn't hate I feel for you
It's love.
These images of you screaming, a slow and painful death.
I cry myself to sleep knowing I could never hate you.

Poem No: 43 'Stars Above'

Watching the stars above
Wishing death would just come over her
Quick and painless
Laying under the stars angry, not with anyone but herself
The lies
The deceit
The games she let go on and on
The lies she told herself to make everything better...
No more tears
No more lies
No more deceit
Lying there wishing on every start
She's not herself.
He took every last ounce of trust she had.
He took everything from her
The lies, deceit, the games
She's closer to the edge; one more step, and she's off
One more step, and she falls to her death.
Watching the stars above
Wishing and hoping.

Poem No: 44 'Anymore'

The pain
The hurt
She can't take anymore
Razor blades
Her wrists
She cuts deep, watching the blood
pour to the floor.
Her blood flows, splashing at her feet
as she cries out in pain.
The tears fall from her eyes and down
her cheeks.
She loves him
She hates him
She's caused more than enough pain
Razors cut deeper, blood flows faster
She falls to the floor as her eyes roll back
Her spirit rises as the blood drains dry from
her lifeless body.
No more pain
No more hurt.

Poem No: 45 'For You'

Watching you
Bleeding for you
Nothing will ever compare to the love
she has for you.
Someone is getting in the way
Her heart beats only for you
She breathes only for you
Nothing can ever compare to what she
has given you.
For so long, she loved you and you alone
The fire inside her burns deep for your
touch.
Waiting for you
Loving you
Nothing will ever compare.

Poem no: 46 'Her Photo'

He looks at her photo
Just a memory of her now
If he could have only seen the pain,
the true pain.
If he could have only really seen, what
she had going on.
The picture falls to the ground as he stumbles.
Nothing is he without her.
He cries out her name.
Only you my heart, he yells
If he only knew
She's just a memory in a photo now.
If he only knew her true pain.

Poem No: 47 'Nobody'

Nobody sees the pain
Nobody cares
She cuts herself deep
Blood drips quickly as death approaches her
Holds out his hand.
They all look on with smiles upon their faces
She cuts one last time before taking death
by the hand and asks,
"Take me, take me far away, please."
Nobody sees the pain
She hides it well
As she walks out and sees nothing's changed
Nobody cares
Nobody realizes just what is going on
Out the door, she walks as she shouts
Good-bye.

Poem No: 48 'The Rivers'

Through the rivers that run from the mountaintops to the
valleys.
Through the stars that rest in the heavens and
Sparkle as bright as the twinkle
In your eyes
My love for you runs deep and true.
Deeper than the deepest part of the ocean.
Truer than the waters that fall from the heavens.
Your touch sends my heart racing faster than ever before.
Your smile sets my soul ablaze.
My body, my ears, my lips, heart and soul crave you,
Crave all of you.
Through the mountaintops to the valleys, the rivers flow
Forever through time and space
Just as my love for you will always be
Forever and true.

Poem No: 49 'Never Knew'

I never knew what I could be, till you came along and opened my heart.

Even when I fall apart, you're still there, holding me together.

The only one who trusts me.

The only one who truly loves me.

You hold your hands out to me

Holding tight, never letting go.

You make me beautiful.

You've shown me how to trust.

You've shown me how to love.

Poem No: 50 'Wanted'

All I've ever wanted,
All I've ever needed:
Just hold me, and never let go.
In your arms is all I want
Your love is all I need
True and deep as the waters run
Open your heart to me.
As I open mine to you.
Wake up and look at what's right in
Front of you.
Open your eyes
Look at what's been standing there
Waiting all this time.
All I've ever wanted
All I've ever needed.
Was your love
Open your soul to me
Let me in, don't leave me in the dark
Just hold me and never let go.
You're what I want, what I need.

Poem No: 51 'Can't Help'

Can't help but smile when I see you.
Can't help but cry when I hear your voice.
You rock my world like no other.
Can't help but laugh at your crazy ways.
Bite my lips and grin when you walk by,
Rock my world, baby.
Mistakes have been made.
Words have been said.
But at the end of the day, all my love is yours.
Can't help but smile when I see you.
Can't help but cry when I hear your voice.
You rock my world like no other.

CPSIA information can be obtained
at www.ICGtesting.com
Printed in the USA
BVHW091229301221
625228BV00014B/920

9 781915 206473